Craig Lancto

Falls the Shadow
and Other Stories

Second Edition

© Craig Lancto 2018

All rights reserved. No part of this publication may be reproduced, stored in a retrieval system, or transmitted in any form or by any means, electronic, mechanical, photocopying, recording or otherwise, without prior written permission from the author.

Good Gnus Press

Shenandoah, Virginia

Also by the author:

from Good Gnus Press

Fighting Ghosts and Chasing the Wind:
The Hero of Talafar

What Do You Do for a Sucking Lip Wound?

Other Works:

Alexandria, Virginia: Where History Lives

Baptism: Gateway to New Life

Banned Books: How Schools Restrict the Reading
of Young People (The World & I)

In and Around the Town of Shenandoah

*Reflections on the Shenandoah (*images)

Thanks to Grayson for keeping me on task.

CONTENTS

For Tina, my stalwart and steadfast friend.

Between the idea
And the reality
Between the motion
And the act
Falls the Shadow

"The Hollow Men"
T.S. Eliot

Falls the Shadow

Albert looked at the hands resting limply in his lap. Old hands, tired hands, wrinkled hands with brown spots and veins bulging as if worms slept under his skin. Hands without hope.

His hands.

He stared with unfocused eyes into the distance and blew out an exasperated breath. "Is this really it? Is this all there is?" Or should he say, "was"?

In his mind's attic, he dusted off a haunting rendition of Peggy Lee's voice: "If that's all there is, my friend, then let's keep dancing...." He hiccuped a sad burst of laughter that took him by surprise.

Maudlin, seems right, he thought.

Melancholy old fool, he thought.

Cliche-ridden, sentimental old fool, he thought.

But he has his work. His work is his life. He snorted a quick sob that forced him to fish a handkerchief out of his back pocket to wipe his nose.

Who still carries a handkerchief?

More than from dark to dark, from well before dawn until well after dark, he worked.

He *liked* his work. It made him happy, gave him a sense of purpose and accomplishment. It gave him a sense of who he was and how others would see him. (And Robbie Burns had a word or two to say about that!)

> *O wad some Power the giftie gie us*
> *To see oursels as ithers see us!*
> *It wad frae mony a blunder free us,*
> *An' foolish notion:*

He is productive and he provides well for his family.

Well, "did." Past tense.

He did provide well, but the boys are grown and have their own families, and Albert is an afterthought—if any kind of thought at all—who gets perfunctory calls on Father's Day and Thanksgiving and Christmas. Usually.

But they are the kind of calls where you can tell that the other person is trying to figure how how soon he can hang up. How long does a phone call have to last to count as "caring"?

Unless the kids are busy, or they forget...or lose interest, then the phone doesn't ring.

Wimoweh, wimoweh

He gave his life for those boys, happily sacrificing to make them happy, to give them every chance of success. Dramatic, yes. I might even give you "melodramatic," but nonetheless true. He happily sacrificed for them, and it worked; they were far more successful than he. They worked less and earned more...so much more. He smiled at how well they have done. Their children are happy–and spoiled. He sighed again and wished that he knew his grandchildren better, had a chance to spoil them himself. He wished that he could see the boys more, especially Billy. The two of them had been inseparable, and the thought that it would not always be so never crossed Albert's mind. And then Billy got engaged and Albert became...what, redundant? Expendable?

Irrelevant.

It hurt profoundly, a dull ache that filled every recess of his soul and no amount of gin seemed enough to drown it out.

When Albert was a boy, his aunts and uncles and cousins, some of them removed a time or two, visited each other at every opportunity. They had family picnics and family reunions, and just seemed to think that hanging with blood was enjoyable. They liked–and wanted to spend time with–each other. When did that change? When did family become a utilitarian unit, raising children as if they were strangers? Strangers who knew their iPads and iPhones intimately, but family not so much.

Favorite movies?

Favorite color?

Eye-roll.

Lame.

Now, the boys–and their families–were not a part of his life in any real sense, so he had only the career he loved and valued.

And then he learned that he was being replaced at work, replaced by a 25-year-old with the ink still wet on her masters in communications. "Fresh ideas and expertise in social media," my Aunt Annie's fanny pack. Cheap replacement is what she is, a scab replacing a non-union employee who wasn't even on strike, is what she is. "A rose by any other name...."

(Her name was not Rose.)

He wasn't sure whether he would rather the boss had not been so direct.

"It isn't you," she assured him. "You have brought your department along faster and further than I ever could have hoped, but you are the highest paid employee we have and we have to cut costs. I can hire someone out of grad school for a fraction of what we're paying you."

And it's a "right to work" state. Gotta love the irony of calling it a "right to work," when what it means is the right for an employer to dump you to hire cheap replacements...to put you out of work. Without cause. More like a "right to not work." The irony is Orwellian.

And now, Dee is leaving.

He spent his life working to give Dee and the boys everything he could, and he actually believed that he and Dee had a good marriage. They never argued; they enjoyed being together. They had fun going out together; they laughed and acted silly together.

You don't act silly with people you don't love—or like, at least.

Dee said that he is not exciting anymore.

"Exciting!"

He never was *exciting*, and they both knew it. Brilliant, witty, charming, sure he admitted to all of these☐maybe too readily☐but *exciting*, is not a word that fits him, *c'est pas le mot juste*.

(Okay, maybe add *affected*.)

So what, after all these years is different?

Brenan.

Brenan is different.

Brenan has a sports car and Brenan has a Harley and Brenan sails and makes her "feel young again."

Brenan.

"He's-just-a-good-friend-at-the-office" Brenan who only asked her to go for a ride in his new sports car because he knew she loves convertibles.

And the next ride was because they had such fun the first time they just wanted to go out again☐and decided to stop for a drink.

Nothing had changed except Brenan's entering stage left, with his floppy blond hair, dimples, long lanky frame, and a smile that melted iron and made the ladies swoon.

One lady, at least.

Well, he isn't *that* tall and some of his mousy, dirty blond hair had retreated from the middle, leaving only the sides and lower back part of his skull protected from the cold. Brenan was not "hot" in any way that Albert could see, but apparently he had won the heart of fair Dee.

And Albert just feels too old and too stale to start over. Certainly too old to be alone–and too alone to want to start over.

He wished her well.

No, really!

He couldn't work up any resentment because he likes her too much, really likes her. He loves her, sure, but he really likes her too. He likes to rub her shoulders and feel her relax under the tenderness of his touch. He likes to hear her sigh as the tension goes out of her. He likes feeling as if love itself was communicated in his touch.

He likes to look at her and to sit beside her, even if they were just reading or watching a movie. She made him—comfortable and content.

So much for comfortable.

And content.

But she seemed happy and they still haven't had an argument really. When she said they had to talk; he asked when she was leaving. (You don't have to be a psychic....) She said "the beginning of the month," and they both kind of nodded like New England farmers talking about the weather.

"Might rain."
"Might.
"Might not, though."
"Noh,"
"Crops could use it."
"Ayuh."
"I'm leaving you for another man."
"Ayuh."
"Need the rain."
"Ayuh."

It was as dramatic as if they had been making plans for the weekend instead of ending the life they knew together.

But inside he was dying. No need for her to know, that. She had made her decision; making her feel bad about it wouldn't help anything; it would just make her feel bad, and he'd feel worse for making her feel bad.

And he'd still be dying inside.

No one wins.

Brenan on the other hand.... Albert wouldn't mind if a truck ran off an overpass and landed flat on Brenan's convertible.

When Dee wasn't in it, though.

God, he loved her. Not like the passionate love he felt thirty years ago, but the love that makes your heart smile and skip a little when she walks into the room. Maybe that's real love, but love on a one-way street is definitely not the love that sonnets make.

Brenan could be in it. Actually, if not, then there's no reason to wreck a perfectly good convertible. Albert likes convertibles. A lot more than he likes Brenan; a lot less than he likes Dee.

So, what should he do?

He knew.

Maybe not "should," but he knew what he would do.

He knew the answer before he asked himself the question.

The boys wouldn't care. At least not much, and not for long.

Dee obviously wouldn't miss him, although he had to believe that she would feel bad…He had to believe that.

Maybe she would miss him, but not enough.

No, there was no doubt. She didn't wish him ill any more than he did her. She only wanted someone more *exciting*, someone more than comfortable and happy. Someone not so "Albert."

He knew what to do, but not how.

Drowning would be hard, all that choking and panic and water up your nose...big time. Even if you want it to happen, that is not the way to go, and he doubted he had the strength of will not to save himself.

That would look like a pathetic cry for sympathy, and he hated pathetic...and sympathy.

Drawing a blade across his wrist? He shivered...an intentional terminal paper cut.

No, that is not the way to go.

Poison? It would probably taste worse than cough syrup, and that is a fate worse than….

Did he have the guts to swallow it? Or to resist calling 911 after he did it?

Dee would see that as another pathetic cry for help. And we already know how he feels about that. He really hated pathetic.

Loves Dee.

A gun?

He couldn't see that happening. He is too spastic to be sure that he would get it right, and it could leave him in worse shape than he is and unable to make a second attempt. Besides, sticking the damn thing in his mouth would make him gag. Then he'd throw up, and who's going to clean up that mess?

Albert laughed at the thought. "Oh, that's good," he said aloud.

"what a delight that you can laugh at the thought of screwing up your own suicide. That could be a sign that you might not be of sound mind."

As if this whole little chat I'm having with myself about topping myself is not.

He laughed again. "Right! Trying to figure out the best way to kill himself is definitely the sign of a healthy mind."

Hanging!
Hmmm. Maybe he'd have an… .
Never mind.
Anyway, don't people soil themselves when they do that?
He'd die of embarrassment.
Another laugh burped between his lips. Self-destruction, what a hoot!
That would make a great book title!
No, he reminded himself. This is serious. Dead serious.
He guffawed. "I kill me!"

He could wrap an ammo belt around his chest and run, screaming, at the White House and let somebody else take care of it.

At bottom, the truth is that, although he is not afraid of dying, he'd rather not be there when it happens.

Albert fell asleep contemplating the least offensive way to seek "that undiscover'd country from whose bourn no traveler returns."

~~~

He awoke as listless as the night before and decided to go for certainty.

If he tried to kill himself and failed, he wouldn't be able to live with himself and then where are you? Alive for starters, the opposite of a successful end, any way you think of it.

"If I slap a noose around my neck and then take some kind of poison before I step out into air, I won't be able to call 911 or have second thoughts.

He nodded in agreement with himself: It is the right thing to do and the right way to do it, he thought. The boys won't care one way or the

10

other, at least not after the first few minutes when they think, 'Dad killed himself? That sucks.'"

He wished that they wouldn't use that expression.

.

Maybe he could….Yeah! He could go to that cliff that overlooks the beach where he and Dee had spent so many evenings walking barefoot in the sand.

We walked together
hand in hand
'cross miles and
miles of golden sand

When he thought they were happy.

But now it's over and
done
'cause that was
yesterday and
yesterday's gone

When he thought that happy was good...at least good enough.
Before she needed someone exciting.
There would be some symmetry in that.

If he did it as the sun was going down, he could savor the symbolism and smell the sea air and see the sky splashed with color as he put the lights out. Maybe have a good cry while he was at it. He hadn't done that yet. He wouldn't cry unless he is about to kill himself; he'd feel weak. But if you can't have a good cry while you go for a space walk with a rope around your neck, what's a heaven for?

Sorry, Robert. I guess that is not the reach you meant.

Albert decided to take the plunge. Literally. To go off the deep end, as it were.

So, does Albert seem depressed enough? Determined enough? To go through with killing himself? How do you think his story ends?

Really! Go ahead: how would you finish this story?

Ready then? Let's see how the author finished it and then you can decide which ending you prefer.

This
    page
        intentionally
          left
            blank
              to
                preserve
                  suspense

(…and deter reading ahead).

Dee scuffed through the sand, feeling the tickle-itch of sand under bare feet for the first time of the summer.

Her feet were as tender as her heart at that moment.

"I love it here," Dee said, hugging herself as she looked out over the sea. As slender as she was, the strong breeze chilled her, even as it blew her long blonde (natural, of course) hair across her eyes.

"I love the smell of the salt air and I love watching the sun slip into the sea. I love the flash of orange sky just before the darkness settles in. That last blast of color before the sun slips away for the night."

She paused in thought, silent thoughts of Albert that appeared unbidden in her memory. She smiled gently, remembering fondly the many times she and Albert had walked hand-in-hand along this stretch of beach. She shook off the thought, unwilling to allow the memory of Albert to cast a shadow over her pleasure in the moment.

She shivered as she sensed a shadow...Then she realized it was an actual shadow.

~~

Albert's eyes started to leak as he pulled the rope out of the trunk. Rat poison in Gatorade seemed like a brilliant idea...as long as it wasn't too diluted to do its work and he could get enough down. He recalled the discomfort of preparing for too many colonoscopies. He had learned to hate Gatorade as he had to force himself to drink what seemed like gallons of the stuff the night before the procedure.

"Maybe I should pour it in the porches of mine ear," Albert said aloud, startled by his voice in the sea breeze...clinging to his appreciation for Shakespeare's work: That guy knew how to write.

He understood people.

He understood death.

And indecision.

To be or not to be....

Yup. That's about right.

He understood so much.

He gets me.

So much learning. So much knowledge. All about to flicker out⬜

14

Out, brief candle.

and

The rest is silence.

If no one else did, Albert appreciated his literary allusions.
No one else did.
He had no illusions.
If anyone else did, he probably wouldn't be here.
But he is.

He looped the rope around his neck and threw the other end over the sturdy limb of the scrub pine at the top of the cliff.. Tying off the rope, he pulled the Gatorade out of the belt pack he carried it in. Not as nerdy as a fanny pack, but a close second, he thought, as he twisted the cap off the plastic bottle.

He closed his eyes, held his breath and slugged it in one go. ...and yup, it reminded him of all the times he'd had to prep for colonoscopy. In a way....

Tossing the bottle aside, (It's not littering; they'll collect it for evidence.) he swung off from the cliff into airy nothingness...and knew immediately why he didn't get a merit badge in knot-tying.

He felt the rope slip and knew that the knot was giving away. The rope constricted his throat and he felt his gorge rise as his legs Wile-E.-Coyoted in the air. In free fall, he knew he was going to vomit...and he did, his final act as he turned face downward and saw the figure walking through the sand below him.

Dee looked up and thought,. "That looks like....

"Dee Hanson. She was dead before she hit the ground," said the medical examiner to the detective who was shaking sand out of his tasseled loafer. "Looks like he landed right on her face. She must have looked up just before he hit."

The detective felt an inappropriate giggle burbling up at the image.

15

"He broke her neck," his partner said, shaking his head, "after vomiting on her and before she butted him in the gut when he landed on her."

He began to smile in spite of himself. How screwed up could one suicide get?

"Yeah, his neck is still raw from the rope, but that was one lucky bastard."

"Lucky?"

"Well, she did break his fall."

"Yeah, but judging by his broken neck, it looks like he was already too dead to appreciate it."

They looked at each other and burst into laughter that quickly grew into belly laughs at the absurdity.

"Of all the freak accidents…"

They regained control and settled their faces back into habitual masks of professional boredom.

A few deep breaths and …

"Well, they're both wearing wedding rings, so we'd better try to find her husband...and his wife."

And now. For a different take!

Christina Richardson has given permission to share her ending to this story, as well. Her version stays true to the style and tone of the original story and provides a very satisfactory alternate conclusion:

Falls the Shadow conclusion By Christina Richardson

Albert sat at the table in the kitchen, hands on either side of his favorite cereal bowl, staring at the fat raisins half submerged in the over-buttered oatmeal. What the hell he thought, "if I am going to do the deed why worry about my cholesterol."

Nothing had changed overnight. He was still brilliant, witty, and charming but would never hear the word *exciting* uttered about him. Unless…

Creativity is the catchword – then the boys would not say 'Dad killed himself? That sucks." Maybe something that is worthy of the Darwin Award would get their attention. Then Dee would wonder if she had misjudged her Albert and that he was exciting after all.

Albert finished his oatmeal, tidied up the kitchen, and booted up the computer in the den to see what inspiration the Darwin Awards had for his exit. Knowing that the Darwin Awards were posthumously awarded to humans who had most creatively removed themselves from the gene pool. Albert spent the morning reflecting on his way of making the top ten for the coming year.

The plan forming slowly in Albert's mind included the cliff that overlooks the beach where he and Dee had spent so many evenings walking barefoot in the sand. The 2004 Mellow Yellow New Beetle convertible that he loved and would never let the boys drive had to be included in the scenario somehow so it too would be part of the story.

By mid-afternoon Albert realized that driving the bug off the cliff, as in the movie Thelma and Louise, was not viable as it had been done and, therefore, lost its uniqueness. Also the cliff was only ten feet in elevation above the beach. It would most likely do a header, nose buried in the sand and rear end mooning the crowds who would scurry over the scene like mice.

Nope – bad idea.

The offing process had started early Monday morning, but it was Saturday of the next week with no plan in place. The internet was proving to be hopelessly inadequate and Albert knew that he was running into a chasm of boring, unimaginative scenarios.

Three weeks later, another Monday morning communing with his raisin infested oatmeal, Albert realized that he had had a very busy month thinking, plotting, planning. It slowly crept up on him that he was having what he tentatively characterized as fun.

All those years, Albert thought, that he had worked to take care of the boys and Dee had been productive and, yes, he had liked what he did and was good at it. He had sacrificed for the boys to give them every chance of success, and it worked; they were happy and successful.

Dee wanted excitement, and all the other things like comfortable, steady, consistent and loving were not enough.

Albert looked at his hands resting on either side of his cereal bowl. Yes they were old hands, tired hands, wrinkled hands with brown spots. They were also hands with fingers and thumbs that had carried him through thousands of hours at the typewriter and then computers.

"Maybe I am not done yet," Albert thought. Maybe there are things these tired old hands can do. Albert headed into the den and booted up his computer, wiggled his rear into that comfortable old cushion on his favorite chair, and hit the keyboard.

August 15, 2009, Albert filled his favorite cereal bowl with his favorite oatmeal and swimming raisins. He opened the *Washington Post* to the book review section.

Book Review: 'PJ, The Yellow Bug, the Next Generation' by Albert Thompson. Reviewed By Kevin Agnew Special to *the Washington Post*.

In 2008 Albert Thompson received the Booker Prize for *PJ, The Yellow Bug*, a postmodern masterpiece that is, in part, the story of a family in crisis and a yellow VW New Beetle convertible that became the hero of a series of children's books for children facing change in their lives. Bristling with life and invention, it is a seductive work by an extraordinarily gifted writer.

Thompson has lived up to his first novel with the sequel, 'PJ the Yellow Bug, The Next Generation.' The original PJ floated off to sea one morning while Thompson was on the beach working on one of the PJ stories.

This new book has all the excitement of the first in the, we hope, series of stories on family dynamics and the search for meaning and hope. Secret passions electrify the stories in this multi-layered autobiographical novel. Following the boys introduced in the first novel we discover that life has not treated them well. Diane, the ex-wife, married her boyfriend of the floppy blond hair, dimples. long lanky frame, and a smile that melted iron and made the ladies swoon. The sports car crashed, the Harley quit running, and Diane, a greeter at a big box department store, drives a Yugo. The no longer blond new husband had left years before. He found a leggy blond with her own sports car.

The energy and excitement of this new book by Thompson will resonate for years to come.

Albert chuckled. "Exciting" is just the word I needed to read.

Breakfast over, Albert called to Desi and Ajax to go for a run with him on the beach. He had never had dogs in his life before. These dog children are happy and spoiled, just like his boys and Dee were. The difference is Desi and Ajax acted like hanging with him was all they wanted to do .

Life is exciting.

Ring around the Rosies
Pocket full of posies

Traditional children's song

All Fall Down

Guadalupé Léon was tending her wilted garden—sparse growth of stringy plants struggling through baked earth—when she saw a gaunt figure trudging toward her. As the figure scuffed along the dusty road, which hardly merited the name, clouds of dust puffed up at each step. It was more of a trail, really, a pair of footpaths that accommodated the rare vehicle, usually a burro cart but even an occasional lost turista in a fancy motor vehicle in quest of ancient ruins.

Her long pigtails, now steel gray shot through with stray strands of ebony, sort of a silver sabled, swayed as she worked, sometimes falling over her shoulders to hang in front of her when she stooped.

She swiped the sweat from the crumpled brown bag of her face with her dust-stained sleeve and squinted at the approaching stranger before returning to her work, hacking at the flinty ground.

Lupé rationed water from her rusting coffee can among the feeble seedlings in the parched earth from which she prodded and coaxed the meager vegetables that added nutrition to her constant diet of beans, rice, and tortillas. She subsisted largely on soups, the most forgiving of foods because she could include beans, wild greens, and roots to eke out her meager crops. But soups meant water, and water meant trudging to the sometimes trickle of a fickle stream, lugging the large bucket that felt as if it weighed as much as Lupé, or making more frequent trips with a smaller container such as the coffee can, a deteriorated souvenir

20

of a visit from her sister Marta when she had made a triumphal return from her relatively affluent life as a chambermaid in America.

Lupé shielded her eyes as she descried the figure, shimmering in the waves of heat radiating from the sun-baked earth, doggedly plodding toward her. As she paused in her work, she thought of her sister and wondered how their ancient mother was faring. When Marta last wrote, the old woman was frail and in ill health.

Lupé did not doubt that taking her to America was best for her mother, but she missed her, and the distance was so much greater than the miles.

As the scarecrow under a battered straw hat drew closer, Lupé felt a brief flash of pleasure as she recognized him as Tomás, her closest neighbor. He rarely walked the three kilometers or so to see her, but occasionally he brought her something that had awaited her in the small store that served double duty as the local post office.

Tomás was little more than a skeleton, his leathery skin seemed a mere coating for his bones. He was a walking mummy in dusty rags. Tomás grinned as he grew closer, a lone tooth catching on his cracked lips. Despite his weariness, he greeted her warmly.

"Buenos días, Señora" he said with the slightest bow in her direction.

Since Luis had died, she knew that Tomás saw a glimmer of hope that his old friend's old wife might become more than his old friend's wizened widow. But, although she genuinely liked the older man, she remained unimpressed by the tooth that stood out so prominently among the row of rotten stumps that lined his black and receding gums.

She braced her lower back with one hand and slowly ratcheted herself into an upright position as she dribbled the last of her water onto her struggling plants.

"Buenos días, Tomás," she answered with a hesitant smile.

"You had a package at la tienda," he said. "From your rich sister in America, I believe."

Lupé reached for the package he extended, its writing as much a mystery to her as to Tomás, but she recognized the labored script that marked letters and packages from her sister.

"Gracias, Tomás," she returned sincerely, "but you should not have walked all this way in such heat."

"It was my great honor, Señora," he said with another shadow of a bow. For knowing her all his life, Tomás was still shy and somewhat in awe of the old widow he remembered as the most beautiful girl within

21

twenty kilometers, pretty much the extent of his world.

"Would you like a cold drink, Tomás?"

"If it is no great trouble, Señora, I would be grateful for something cool."

"Rest here in the shade and I will fetch some water.

Guadalupé turned and walked more briskly than her protesting bones would like toward the small stream that provided her only source of water. She knew that Tomás would be watching her, and even if she was not interested in him, she liked knowing that he found her attractive.

Tomás stretched out in the scant shade provided by the scrubby tree next to Lupé's garden and covertly watched her under the broken brim of his straw hat as she trudged toward the stream. Perhaps he should have offered to accompany her, but the long walk had been tiring in such heat.

He must have dozed because he was suddenly aware that Guadalupé was saying something to him. His conscious mind merged with a very pleasant dream in which she was saying sweet nothings, but as he swam toward the surface of wakefulness, he realized that she was standing in front of him holding a metal cup.

"Your water, Tomás," she said smiling.

"I am sorry, Señora. I was...deep in thought."

They locked eyes and both laughed quietly at the thin lie.

"Have you received something wonderful from your sister?" he asked, hoping that he might share in the bounty and stay a little longer with Lupé.

"Oh, I have not yet had a chance to look," she said. "Come, we will see what she has sent."

The old pair shuffled toward her hovel, the dirt floor meticulously neat, and Tomás sat at one of the two painted chairs at the battered wooden table, while lupé examined the package.

Wrapped in brown paper, the package was the size of a large baby's head and not especially heavy. Accepting the knife that Tomás constantly wore on the rope that kept his ragged trousers from tripping him, lupé cut through the outer wrapping and encountered—more paper. The inner wrap was waxier, like the butcher paper, which Guadalupé had seen on one of her exciting excursions to the city as a young woman. It bore additional writing, no less mysterious to lupé and Tomás than the address itself had been.

She asked Tomás to cut away the rest of the wrapping and found herself staring at a cardboard box with yet more indecipherable markings.

Inside the box, she found a sealed tin with writing that included what she recognized as the name of her mother.

"It is a gift from my mother!" she exclaimed happily. Tomás looked quizzically from the container to Lupé's glowing face.

With a gesture, his friend extended the package to him and said, "Please?"

Tomás prized open the container and they both peered curiously into a gritty, grayish powder, with some larger, unidentified bits in the mix.

"What is it?" asked Tomás, mystified.

"I don't know," said Lupé, sniffing at the contents and examining the container from all sides.

"From time to time Marta sends me small American treats, but usually the package shows a picture of what is inside."

"My favorite is small packets with a picture of a glass pitcher on the front. It makes water wonderful with fruit flavors. Well, not very fresh fruit, perhaps, but when I have sugar cane the drink is sweet and very delicious."7+

"Sometimes, she sends me powders that make hot chocolate, even some with tiny pieces of white sweets floating in them." Her face glowed as she savored the memory.

"Sometimes she sends me packets with pictures of different kinds of soups, and when I add them to hot water, they make the most delicious meals."

"Perhaps this is such a powder?" suggested Tomás, hoping that he would be invited to try one of these tasty North American delicacies.

"I suppose we could boil some water and see what happens," returned Guadalupé, again sniffing at the contents. "Most powders mix better in hot water, and if it seems something that would be better cold, we can just let it cool and try it later." Truth be told, this box did not exude any of the usual exciting scents of drink mixes or soups. It smelled earthier, more like dried mushrooms, perhaps, powdered mushrooms?

Tomás shrugged noncommittally, but he was pleased at the promise of "we."

He studied the box while Guadalupé went to the stream for more water, but it yielded up no more secrets no matter how intensely or from what angle he looked at it. He too sniffed gingerly at the contents, but to no more avail than his friend.

23

While Guadalupé stoked the small fire and boiled water, the two shared the limited gossip of such a remote area. When the water was ready, Lupé measured a few teaspoons of the coarse powder into two cups of steaming water. She could detect no distinct smell, although it had a distinctly earthy, almost muddy, scent. A tentative sip was not encouraging.

The mixture looked pale, she thought, deciding to add more to see if she could recognize what it is. Her sister would certainly not have sent it if it wasn't something special. Maybe it was some sort of healthy drink; in her limited experience, the better it is supposed to be for your health, the less likely a chance that one would enjoy drinking it.

When the mixture had darkened, she decided that it must be ready. The earthy smell was stronger, but the scent revealed nothing. She still wasn't certain whether it was a powdered drink or soup or something more exotic.

Tomás sipped from the cup Guadalupé offered him and pulled a face.

"This is…not familiar," he said thoughtfully…and diplomatically.

Trying her own, Lupé grimaced, "No," she said slowly. "It is not very pleasant."

"No," said Tomás. "It is not."

"It must have a different use," said Lupé. "I must think about how else to use it."

Tomás left without finishing his drink.

As much as Guadalupé tried— in honor of her mother—she could not do so either, but rather than waste the precious fluids, she poured them on the parched plants in her garden and returned the mystery box to a shelf.

Over the next week or so, Guadalupé tried adding the mixture to other dishes, but found that it added nothing. In truth, it left a heavy, somewhat unpleasant taste, and it was gritty, almost like eating sand.

So, here we are again. Before reading on, how do you think this story ends? What is supposed to be so good about this box's unimpressive contents that Lupé's sister would send it to her from the United States?

Before reading how the author concludes this story, take a few minutes to write how you think the story ends.

Tell me when you're ready.

Okay? Great. Let's read the author's ending and you can decide which is better.

Sweeping out her shack one day, she again saw a cloud of dust moving toward her faster than someone walking...certainly faster than Tomás. As he approached,Lupé saw that it was the boy who sometimes helps the old man at the tienda, wobbling along on an ancient bicycle with fat balloon tires and white walls that had chipped away in spots.

When the boy arrived, he allowed his bicycle to drop on the parched ground, puffing up sprays of dust. In his hand he held letter.

"Good morning, Señora," he said. "Sr. DeSilva said that I was to bring you this letter—that it is muy importante," the boy added gravely.

Although she could not read the letter she stared at the words, the boy as curious—and illiterate—as she, but the mystery remained unsolved.

Had she been able to read the letter, the mystery would still not have been revealed because, although she would understand "Mama," the word "cremains" would have held no meaning for her.

There will be time, there will be time
To prepare a face to face the strangers that you meet....

"The Love Song of J. Alfred Prufrock"
T.S. Eliot

Among Strangers

Ben hurried into the auditorium for his history final. He had skipped too many classes and too many readings, but the professor had personally reviewed what would be on the exam. With Professor Kaplan, seeing the man himself instead of a teaching assistant was like seeing Halley's Comet. For Ben, this exam was living the dream...the one in which he takes an exam for which he hasn't studied or attended lectures. In his underwear.

Ben loathed these lecture classes where the professor makes a guest appearance once or twice a semester while nerdy teaching assistants drone through the lecture notes. More than once he had thought that the least a full professor—even one as obnoxious and arrogant as Kaplan—could do would be to record the classes one time so they could have the benefit of the expertise he is paid for instead of sending in the second string. Then students could record the recording and everyone could stay home.

He looked around the room, recognizing almost no one. Partly because of his...shall we say imperfect?...attendance, but also because, with hundreds of college students in an auditorium, it's hard to really get to know anyone.

For Ben, spotty attendance was not for the usual college reasons...too much party and not enough sleep or too much sorority

27

sister...and not enough sleep. Ben often missed class because he had overslept, but not for any of the fun reasons. He had to work to pay the many expenses not covered by his veteran's benefits: food, rent, diapers....

It was never his plan to have a baby, but when he learned that his girlfriend was pregnant, he had no choice. She was as vehemently opposed to motherhood, as he is to abortion, so they compromised. She carried the baby to term, but *his* religious beliefs didn't mean that *she* had to hang around.

And she didn't.

Ben was okay with that. He would prefer that his son have two parents, but he was absurdly proud of the little guy and madly in love with him. Ben figured that one doting parent is better than two, if one of them resents the baby. Alison did not gather dust arguing the point.

Ben knew that getting a college degree meant not only a better job, but also a better life for him and for Michael. He was determined to do whatever it takes to give Michael the best life he possibly could. And even though he had had a week or so when Michael had kept him awake crying all night with a deadly combination of colic and his first tooth coming in, and sleep was just a pipe dream, he had found a new and profound satisfaction in simply holding and caring for his baby, flesh of his flesh, blood of his blood. He found Michael amazing, and when he stared into his son's deep blue eyes so like his own, he felt as if he were falling into them. Michael's giggle suggested that he felt it, a deep connection to the man he knew loved him.

Ben was smiling to himself at the thought of his son, but his reverie was broken when teaching assistants began passing out blue books, and Ben quickly read through his study notes one more time. He was pretty sure that he had it. Even if he had cruised through the semester, he had done some serious studying for the past week and believed that he knew the material cold. He was ready.

As the teaching assistants began passing out the exam, Professor Kaplan used the microphone:

"All right, everyone, we are passing out the exams, so you will need to stop talking and clear everything off your desks except blue books and test questions.

"This is a timed test, so leave your questions face down until we tell you to begin.

"You will have exactly two hours to complete the exam. At the end of that time, we will tell you to stop writing and to place the test questions inside your blue books, and to pass them to the end of the row.

"Do not leave your seats until all test booklets have been collected."

When the assistants had finished passing out the tests, Kaplan made a great show of studying his Rolex before announcing, "And... begin."

Ben wrote furiously. Studying had paid off. He was elated to realize that not only did he know the answers, but he also was able to elaborate on them at length.

He looked around and saw that many of the other students were staring into space for the answers, or gnawing worriedly at their pencils. He was giddy with pleasure that he was doing so well.

But when Kaplan announced that ten minutes remained, Ben realized, to his horror, that he had written so much in some answers that he was a long way from finishing. And although he didn't know Kaplan well, he knew him well enough to know that he considered students an impediment to his publishing and tennis. He tolerated the graduate students who did most of the work for his books and articles, but his contempt for undergraduates was renowned. And Ben, who had returned to college after four years of military service, was subjected to supplemental scorn because he was not a traditional student who was easily bullied. Attending a college near a large army base meant that he was one of a number of veterans taking the required course.

Ben heard some students toss their pencils down as they felt the end of the time approach.

When Kaplan told them to put down their pencils, Ben tried furiously to finish one more answer.

The professor's eye found him.

"I said 'time.' Now. Put down your pencil."

Ben scrawled the rest of his sentence and put down his pencil.

"Place your test questions inside your blue book. Be sure your name is on the cover of each of the blue books you have used—and pass your tests to the center aisle,...except the young man in the ...five, six, seven, eight...tenth row."

Ben looked up, his face flushed with shame, embarrassment, and anger.

"Yes, you. You may keep yours as a reward for continuing to write past the deadline."

"It wasn't even a minute, Professor..." Ben protested.

"It *was* a minute more than the allotted time," Kaplan responded with a smirk. "Rules are rules. If I make an exception for you, then everyone else could just finish when he felt like it."

Ben felt his face flush with embarrassment...and anger. For once, Ben was happy that no one knew him. He felt humiliated and frustrated. Never confident in his academic abilities, returning to college had been a difficult decision. Following through while providing for himself and his baby, made it more so. He didn't need this.

He watched as the other students, many casting sidelong glances at him, passed in their books.

The teaching assistants stacked them on the table in the front of the room, stealing furtive glances at Ben, who was lingering after the students were dismissed.

Oops. Sorry to interrupt, but I'll bet you were expecting it this time.

So, poor Ben, am I right? He didn't deserve that treatment. Or maybe he did; the rules were clear.

So, the only question here is how you think the story ends. Go ahead, finish it your way and then see how the author did it.

Waiting....

Ready? Okay, let's see how the other version ends:

Ben walked to the front of the auditorium instead of toward the exits, Professor Kaplan watching him balefully as he approached.

As he reached the table, Kaplan said, "There's no use arguing your case. In this class I am the court of last resort. You violated my rules and you will pay the penalty." The smirk again. Ben hated his smug satisfaction.

He gazed silently at the man, deciding how best to handle the situation. Then he drew himself up and took a deep breath.

"Professor, do you have any idea who I am?" he asked.

"I do not," Kaplan admitted, his lip actually curling with disdain. "And I am happy to say that it wouldn't matter if you were the university president. You'd still have no recourse."

"Good," Ben said, swiftly thrusting his blue books into the center of the pile of test books that he sent sprawling on the floor.

He strode out of the auditorium, grinning in response to the red-faced professor's apoplectic demands for him to return, this instant.

My secrets cry aloud.
I have no need for tongue.
My heart keeps open house,
My doors are widely swung.

from "Open House"
Theodore Roethke

Open House

Gary braked to a stop in his driveway. He exhaled a long breath, relieved that the tiring drive was safely over. He turned off the engine and headlights, but before the engine could tick more than twice, he turned his lights on once again. Something looked wrong. Possibly the subtle shift in shadows on his front door. Although one typically is not conscious of memorizing the smallest details, after years of pulling into the same driveway, his eyes had grown accustomed to the subtlest of changes. Now it looked different, but he couldn't distinguish precisely how.

He doused the lights again and climbed slowly out of the car, sending his family across the street to stay with neighbors while he investigated. "Listen," he said quietly, "Why don't you all go over and wish the Dolans a Merry Christmas while I go in and turn the lights on."

Eager to see what Santa brought, the children murmured dissent; their mother gave Gary a questioning look, but a tacit signal told her to do as he suggested.

Collecting his overnight bag from the floor of the backseat, he approached his house with caution.

The coach light at his door glowed softly in the misty evening. Inside, he could see the living room lamp that turns on automatically at the same time every evening. A second lamp in the den would turn itself on in about 45 minutes. A third, upstairs in the master bedroom, was scheduled to turn itself on and then off again after another 45 minutes. He had staggered the lamps so that they did not look quite so automatic. The television was also set to turn on in time for the news, and then off two hours later. Gary believed that his preparations had been very clever.

He slowly climbed the front steps, and as he reached the landing he saw that the front door, had been forced, even though it was now closed.

He groaned in recognition. This was not the first time that he had been burgled, not even the first time in the past six months. And last Christmas they had taken all of the gifts from under the tree. Their friends told Gary that they would have to use that excuse the next gift-giving season.

He found that his key worked in the second lock, but even as he felt the click, he felt the door begin to push open at his pressure. Before him, the hall closet door was open and he could see that clothes had been thrown to the floor, some still on hangers.

He closed the front door quietly and stepped into the room, ears pricked for the slightest sound.

He held his breath, listening intently. Quietly setting his bag on the floor, he began to move into the living room, sensing that whoever had been there was gone.

With a glance though the darkened dining room into the unlighted kitchen, he climbed the stairs to the second floor and peered into the master bedroom, his bedroom. The first thing he noticed was that dresser drawers had been pulled out, the contents roughly tossed, and pushed partially back in. Then, the half-open closet door.

He approached gingerly. The bedroom closet was a replay of the hall closet downstairs: clothes thrown on the floor, box lids askew. The top shelf was in disarray. Oddly, he didn't see that anything seemed to be missing.

Each of the bedrooms was the same: dresser drawers open and mussed; closets open, clothes thrown to the floor, contents scattered about. And nothing obviously missing.

Returning to the first floor, he passed cautiously through the dining room and kitchen to the basement stairs. At the bottom, he turned on the lights and saw nothing amiss. Moving to the back room, he found that the trash bags he had stored near the cellar door had been slashed open, the contents spilling onto the floor. Still, nothing seemed missing.

Gary returned to the kitchen, hands on hips as he surveyed the wreckage. Three previous times in the past six months, he had come home to find that he had been burgled. He picked up the phone to call the police—again—when he heard someone at the door.

~~~~~

Four months earlier.

It was a hot summer night, humid and uncomfortable, but Gary finally had fallen into a fitful sleep. A light breeze gently moved the curtains at his bedroom window. His family had gone to the lake for the weekend, but he had work and stayed at home.

The floorboards creaked, quietly enough, but sufficient to awaken Gary from his shallow sleep. He remembered clearly and immediately that he should be alone. He turned over and opened one eye. He thought that he caught movement, where the darkness was thicker. He moved slightly to use peripheral vision instead of trying to focus straight on. The figure of a man tiptoeing across his bedroom, almost mime-like in his movements slowly took shape. Without conscious thought, Gary threw back the covers and leapt out of bed. The figure turned and fled, Gary close behind in silent chase.

The intruder pounded along the upstairs hallway, Gary almost at his heels. Around the column and down the stairs, ever in silence beyond the sound of pounding feet the two raced. As the figure bounded from the landing and dashed into the dining room, it dawned on Gary that he was unarmed. Moreover, he realized, he had no idea whether the intruder was. He slowed his pace.

In the kitchen the intruder hooked a left to the basement stairs and Gary stopped at the wall phone to dial 911.

"9--1-1. What is your emergency?"

"There's someone in my house," he shouted.

"Someone is there now?" asked the 911 dispatcher.

"Yes! I have him cornered in the basement; I am at the top of the stairs."

"Are you somewhere safe?"

"I'm in the kitchen. I chased him into the basement."

35

"Assistance is on the way, sir. You need to find someplace safe. If you can, get out of the house. Please stay on the line."

Gary was astonished at the speed of the response. Even as he went to the front of the house, he saw a patrol car pulling up. Despite the rash of burglaries, he lived in a good neighborhood. He was surprised that the police were so near.

When the first officer came to the door, hand on his sidearm, nGary opened the door and the gun came up almost instantly as the officer's eyes widened.

Noting that it was unlikely that an intruder would answer the door...in his shorts... (especially *those* shorts!) the officer moved quickly past Gary into the house, his fellow officers close behind him.

He could hear the squawk of police radios as additional units arrived.

"He's in the basement, Gary whispered, "to your left when you enter the kitchen." Police were filing in to the house like a trail of armed ants.

"You need to stay out of the way," an officer told him.

Gary went out the back door onto the deck, where he saw strobing lights from additional police cars on the street behind his house. Officers with flashlights were approaching from several directions.

From the deck, he could not see that the external basement door beneath him was open. It was the way the intruder had broken in. It was the way the intruder had left, even as Gary was on the phone with police dispatch.

Nothing seemed to be missing, and Gary felt that he had dodged a bullet. He hoped not literally.

~~~~~

A month later, Gary came home from work and went to deposit his change in his coin bank, a ceramic monk with a fringed tonsure and a coin slot in his back. "Thou shalt not steal" was emblazoned in script across his chest.

The house seemed very still. Laura was still at work and the children at day care.

He stood with his hand hovering over his dresser...where his monk bank used to be. It wasn't there. Neither was it on the floor behind or under the dresser. Neither was his jewelry box, filled with cuff links and tie tacks, his college ring and the ruby ring his father had passed on to him from *his* father. Further search revealed that his digital recorder and a few other small items also had gone missing.

He called the police and they asked a few questions, took his list of missing property gave him an incident number and said that they would be in touch. They both knew that this was the last time they would discuss such small potatoes.

A year ago.

The weekend before Christmas, Gary and his family went to visit his parents, planning to return Christmas morning for the children to open their gifts, which had been arranged around the tree like so many boulders at the foot of a waterfall and extending well into the room.

They tumbled out of the car and scrambled to the front door, excited at the prospect of getting into the house to see what Santa had left.

No one was more surprised or disappointed than Gary when they rushed into the house to find a few bows and some wrapping paper where the presents had been. His children stared up at him in wide-eyed disappointment.

Once again, the basement door, hidden at the bottom of stairs below ground at the back of the house, had been the Achilles' door. Its frame was shattered and splinters hung from the deadbolt installed after the first time he had been burgled.

It was difficult explaining to the children, and friends whose gifts had disappeared along with the children's, teased him that they would have to remember to use the same excuse the next year.

The police spent about an hour in his house, but Gary sent the rest of the day with all-purpose cleaner and a roll of paper towels, wiping fingerprint powder from the doors, door jambs, light switches and walls.

Ho, ho, #$%^*& ho.

~~~~~

Enough! Gary nailed shut the back door and installed hardware to hold a think plank across it to preclude its being breached again. He

37

also installed timers on several lamps and asked the neighbors to keep an eye on the house when he was away.

It was a few months before the family again ventured away overnight, and Gary felt uneasy about leaving the castle undefended. After three burglaries in a little more than a year, he felt under siege.

Neighbors reported similar break-ins, although fewer, and the neighborhood had become hypervigilant against the onslaught, offering some degree of assurance.

So now Gary was chagrined to see that the front door was closed but damaged and ajar.

Chagrined! He thought he was going to vomit.

He sent his family across the street for safety--they were used to it by now--and told them to call the police. He gingerly entered and began an inventory of damage and destruction, beginning with the hall closet.

The door was open and clothes had been removed and thrown on the floor. Other closets also showed that they had been ransacked, and in the basement storeroom, he found trash bags waiting to go to the curb slit open, their contents spilled onto the floor.

But when he heard people enter, it was not the police; it was his family and the Dolans from across the street who filed in silently, as after a death in the family..

His family quietly took seats in the living room, Mrs. Dolan remained standing. When Gary reappeared, perspiration glistened on the surface of his face, flushed red, with veins popping in his forehead.

"They got us again," he said in exasperation. "Nothing missing, but the house ransacked."

Gary sat and leaned forward, head in his hands. "I don't know why they bother," he said. "Anything worth taking is long gone."

"Gary," his neighbor said, her voice unsteady, her one dead eye staring at his right ear. "I am so sorry."

He looked at her, one eyebrow raised in question.

"I wish that you had told me that you put timers on the lights. When I saw them go on and I knew that you were out of town, I called the police."

"But..." he glanced toward the ransacked closet in the hallway and back at his neighbor, whose face confirmed her guilt and regret.

"I'm so sorry," she repeated.

"But, why...?"

Gary's face turned from angry frustration to confusion.

The Dolans returned home, heads hanging, although they clearly had done nothing wrong.

Gary phoned the police.

"I understand why they broke in when they had a report of an intruder, but why ransack my closets and slit open the trash bags?" he asked.

"Sir," the officer replied, "Officers had to check the closets quickly for their own safety. Someone could have hidden behind the clothes, so they dumped them as quickly as possible to be sure that no one was there. As they went through the house, they repeated the procedure in each room."

"But the trash bags?" he asked. It was as close to a whine as he chose to approach.

"The bags could have contained stolen goods, sir. They wanted to check because if they did contain stolen goods it would indicate that the burglars were still present or planning to return. It was faster to cut the bags than to untie the twists."

"I see," he said, deflated. "Thank you."

Gary opened a bottle of dry red wine, took a glass from over the bar and went to his study, where he sat in the dusky twilight drinking the wine without tasting it, and wondering what he had done to bring this chronic misery on himself and his family. Sleep came just about when he found the bottom of the bottle.

While Gary catches a little nap, let's stop here and think about how we are going to get out of this story. If I tell you that it is based on actual events....well, it is based on actual events. That doesn't mean that your version of the story has to end as prosaically as the actual version--or have I said too much?

Okay, how would you end this story?

Tell me when you're finished.

Really, you're not going to try?

Okay, one way or the other, here is how the story originally ended:

This
    page
       also
            intentionally
              left
                blank
                  to
                    preserve
                      suspense

(…and deter looking ahead).

Although there was a decline in the number of break-ins in the neighborhood, four or five houses including Gary's suffered repeated intrusions. It was as if the burglar or burglars knew when they were vulnerable, knew when the houses were unoccupied.

Some months later, Gary's next-door neighbor's son called from school. He had forgotten his gym suit and wanted Rick, his father, to bring it to him.

Rick dropped the suit off at the school, about a mile away, and returned quickly.

When he entered his living room, he heard a noise in the basement, a thump as if someone had slammed something--or slammed into something. He went to his gun safe and retrieved and loaded his nine millimeter before investigating.

Descending the stairs into the basement, he heard someone scrambling near the furnace.

"I have a gun and I am not afraid to use it," he announced. "Come out of there with your hands where I can see them."

Silence.

"I'll count to three and then it's all on you," he said.

"One…."

"No. Wait, I'm coming out. Don't shoot, man. I ain't got nuthin'."

"Keep your hands where I can see them. Make sure they are empty."

The first thing he saw emerging from the shadows behind his furnace was the whites of eyes, like glowing saucers. The he noticed the trash bag near the basement door.

The man who emerged looked vaguely familiar.

"Upstairs," Rick said, motioning with his gun.

The man walked dejectedly before him to the kitchen and kept his hands up as Rick called 911.

While they waited for the police—which was not more than two minutes—Rick said. "I know you. At least I've seen you."

Of course he had, as he realized once the police arrived and identified the man. He lived in the house behind a high fence to the rear and between Rick's and Gary's houses. With a long record of petty crimes, he was a holdout in the one run-down house that had escaped neighborhood gentrification. From his second floor bedroom, he could watch the homes of his more affluent neighbors in the rehabbed homes that surrounded him, and he could move quickly in and out when he saw everyone leave home. It explained why these houses had been hit so often and without detection.

Rick's less-than-ten-minute trip to the middle school was shorter than the intruder had bargained for and it was the undoing of an almost perfect plan to make money for his drug habit while he punished the rich (He thought.) people who had invaded his neighborhood.

And now, his home also is vacant, although it has remained unviolated…other than the workmen renovating it for auction.

A certain man went down from Jerusalem to Jericho,
and fell among thieves,

Luke 10:30

From Jerusalem to Jericho

"Is there significance to the fact that the parable of the Prodigal Son is the longest in the Bible?" asked Brett Larson, an earnest young theology major.

"Probably because it is the critical and central message of Christianity," The handsome young priest responded. His youth and muscularity helped students to identify with him, some to fantasize about him—in a biblical way—and some to wish to emulate him, not necessarily as a priest, but as an affable, unpretentious, intellectual, and athletic role model. Who happened to be an Adonis.

"Like the parable of the Lost Sheep and the parable of the Lost Coin, it is a lesson on the overarching importance of redemption. These parables are not one-dimensional stories, but profound lessons with layers of understanding directly applicable to our lives. Think on them and apply them to our contemporary world—specifically to your life—and you will have no problem with the final exam. And that's no parable; it's fact."

The students laughed quietly and talked among themselves as they left Father Jankowsi's class. It was always a favorite because he brought the bible to life, leading students to consider parables as more than literature, more even than religious tracts, but as timeless models for life. Without being remotely preachy, Father Jankowski led his students to look for spiritual truth and how it manifests itself in our actions. how to integrate the bible's guidance into their own lives.

They murmured about his final exam, always reportedly unique.

"He'll probably give us a forced choice,' said Marge Butler, a slightly overweight young woman with a plain face and hair that appears to be chopped short at home before having dust rubbed into it. Her mind is second to none. "Who is more deserving in the sight of God, the tax collector or the Pharisee, the prodigal son or the faithful servant?"

"Adolf Hitler or Osama bin Laden; George W. Bush or George H.W Bush," suggested the typically sardonic Adam Nard, a gangly Uriah Heep of a fellow, typically dressed in melancholy black, whether echoing sacerdotal garb or paying homage to Johnny Cash never quite clear. His adams apple was so prominent as to threaten unbalancing him and toppling him onto his beak of a nose.

"No," Larry said. A clichéd ginger with enough freckles for endless creative dot-to-dot games, Larry was cursed with eternal optimism. "I think he'll do something like he did a few years ago, give each of us an imaginary $1,000 and ask us to show how we would safeguard it, or grow it, like the parable of the Servants and the Talents in Matthew."

"You're both wrong," said Rick. "He'll make us all strip naked as the day we are born and send us out to spend a day considering the lilies of the field."

"You've been looking for an excuse to do that," said Chris.

The group laughed.

"No. I have it!" Marge said. "He is going to make it a winner-take-all and we have to apply it to the Pearl of Great Price."

It was a gorgeous spring day, sunny with a gentle breeze, as the students made their way to Lincoln Hall for their exam. But they found the door locked with a note that they should instead meet at the Tabard, a café on campus, at 9:30, about a half-hour away.

As they hurried across campus to the café, they talked excitedly about the meaning of meeting at a café.

"If we have to change water into wine…I'm just going to get drunk," said Chuck.

"Too obvious—and blasphemous," said Celia. "It has to be some kind of a moral dilemma; he wouldn't expect miracles."

"You mean, more like Coke into Pepsi or Pepsi into Coke?" Jean asked.

Their banter was silenced at the sight of a young man sprawled supine on the ground near the walkway.

"Speaking of drunk," said Larry. "I hope he doesn't have any exams today."

The group laughed uneasily, and hurried on to the pub.

"You think he's okay?" Chuck asked.

The group paused, uncertain about what to do. They'd feel silly if he was just catching a quick nap between classes, but if he were sick or hurt...

"He might be hurt." Rick said, hesitantly.

"It looks to me as if he started celebrating end of semester a little early. Anyway, we are going to be late for Father Jankowski."

"Well, if anybody'd understand....I'm just going to check, okay? It'll take two secs."

"Okaaay," said Marge. "I'll tell him you're on your way."

Rick walked to the man lying on the grass, while his classmates continued to the cafe in awkward silence. A few looked back uncertainly.

"Excuse me?" he said, tentatively.

"Excuse me?" slightly louder. "Hello?" He looked around, uncertain about how—or whether—to proceed.

Around him people were scurrying to their own exams, appointments, tennis.... No one was paying any attention.

As Rick leaned closer to the man, he saw what appeared to be blood at the corner of his mouth.

He touched his shoulder. "Hey, are you okay?"

Nudging him gently, he repeated: "Hey, bud, are you all right?"

With no response, he felt panic—a sick, sweaty feeling with high blood pressure—take hold.

"Hey! Are you all right?"

He gently turned him over and the body opened one eye. He looked as if he had fallen face first out of a tree.

Rick knelt and cradled the stranger's head in his lap. "Are you okay? What happened?"

"I got jumped," he mumbled through broken lips. "They got my wallet ... and my hoodie... and just kept beating on me—and laughing."

Rick wasn't sure what to say.

"Is anything broken? I mean ribs or anything."

The other man groaned and gingerly began testing parts of his body.

46

"I don't think so, but I feel like a broken maraca."

Rick snorted a laugh. "Well, what can I do? Do you want me to call the campus police?"

"No. They'll never find them anyway. I never really saw them. Either they had a fist in my eye or I was doubled over from a gut punch. Either way, eye contact wasn't on my top ten list of things to do while they were working me over."

"How about the infirmary? You should probably get checked out."

"No, but thanks. I have to get to my physics exam or I'm going to be here for another year."

Rick looked around again. No one else seemed to notice them as they hurried on their way.

"Listen, we're not far from The Tabard. Let me get you there; you can something to eat and drink and rest a little before your exam."

"No, man. I appreciate it but I'm okay. When you came over I was just thinking I hurt too much to move, but when I actually did, it wasn't as bad as I thought."

"I'd feel better if you came to the café for something to drink at least."

"Thanks, man. That's cool." He stuck out his hand. "I'm Jason, but you're forgetting, my wallet…."

Rick took his hand. "Rick. And if you can make it, we'd better get going."

Jason winced as Rick helped him to his feet, but once they started walking, he felt himself loosen up. "At least I didn't lose any teeth, and I should get my beauty back in a few days." He laughed feebly.

When they reached the café, Father Jankowski was nursing a cup of coffee at one of the window tables.

"I'm sorry I'm late, Father. I just had to… Where is everybody?"

"First things first, Rick" said the priest. "Who is your friend?"

"Sorry, Father. This is Jason." He turned to look. Jason was sitting slumped at a table near the restrooms.

"Say, Father, can you just give me another minute?"

"Why not, I've already waited ten."

Rick swasn't sure whether to thank him or apologize and quickly looked again to gauge the priest's mood.

"Thanks, Father. I'll be right back."

Rick strode to the counter. "Iced coffee and an apricot Danish, please." He paid the counterman and said, "Listen, here's another ten. If that guy—his name's Jason—needs anything else. He doesn't have any money with him."

The counterman nodded and Rick carried the coffee and sweet to Justin.

Setting them on the table. He asked, "How are you feeling?" Jason lifted his head and smiled. "Fine, man. You have been great. I don't know how to thank you."

Rick smiled and shrugged. "Just take care of yourself, okay?"

Jason nodded.

"I know you don't have any money or anything, so if you want another coffee or something, just tell the counter guy and he'll take care of you.

He scribbled on a paper in his notebook. "And if you need anything, let me know. Here's my cell number."

Returning to the priest's table, he sat down. "I'm really sorry I missed the exam. Is there any way I can make it up?"

Ha! A snowball's chance in….

Well, you know the drill by now. Will Father J. allow Rick to make up the exam or tell him it's a life lesson in meeting responsibilities?

I guess it doesn't have to be forced choice, you could choose c) none of the above and come up with something original. That would be lovely, wouldn't it.

I'll wait over here with a an egg cream while you figure it out.

Back already? Okay, tell us what you got and then we'll check out what the fella who originally wrote the ending thought happened. (I sincerely hope yours is better than that one.)

Alrighty, then, here we go:

Father Jankowski smiled: "You have nothing to make up."

He nodded toward Jason, who waved in return, looking decidedly brighter. As they watched, the young seminarian stood and walked briskly toward the men's room to wash away the stage blood.

The priest smiled and said,."'A certain man went down from Jerusalem to Jericho, and fell among thieves....' You did well, son. I hope to see you in another of my classes." With that Father Jankowski stood and left the café. Confused, Rick turned to where Jason had been sitting, but –except for the counterman, the place was deserted.

Hell is full of good meanings,
but heaven is full of good works.

Albanian Proverb

An excuse is worse and more terrible than a lie,
For an excuse is a lie guarded.

Pope John Paul II

The Road to Hell

The idea of a pilgrimage had appealed to both of them as they planned their first trip to Europe, visiting the Vatican in Rome and making a detour to visit Lourdes in France. In their—ahem—golden years, they were grateful for their excellent health. Oh, she had trouble with her ankles and he with his knees, but, they joked, the first 80 years are the hardest—and they still had healthy elbows.

The old woman savored the bright spring sun on her face as she dozed in her wheelchair. Pilgrims passed by, to and from the healing waters of Lourdes. Her husband looked lovingly at her and smiled as he walked the short distance to purchase a small phial of the water as a souvenir of their pilgrimage to the renowned grotto. Maybe he'd even rub a little behind his knees. Couldn't hurt, right?

As he studied the coins in his hands in preparation for paying he heard the panicked shouts of a woman who sounded very much like his wife. Turning to seek the source of the commotion, he was stunned to see a young boy in a Scout uniform briskly pushing his wife along the bridge. It was her shouts that had drawn his attention, as another boy seemed to speak earnestly to his wife of more than 50 years.

"Mabel" he shouted and began running toward the wheelchair as fast as his arthritic knees would carry him.

"Stop!" he called again but his cry was interrupted by one of surprise as he tripped over a stone and fell hard to the ground, his head bouncing once off the packed earth. A crowd quickly gathered around his immobile body as his wife's wheelchair bounced to a stop. The Scouts who had been with the boy pushing his wife retraced their steps to see whether they could offer first aid to the fallen man. Mabel grabbed her chest and tried to call for help, but she felt faint, her chest fluttered as if filled with butterflies.

Trying to stand, she collapsed on the ground, her face near a pile of fresh excrement left by a white miniature poodle.

Fellow pilgrims rushed to her assistance, drawing the attention of the Scouts who stopped their headlong rush at the shout behind them.

Looking at each other, they pivoted and returned to help the woman who had fallen from the wheelchair, but when the first reached her side, his foot slipped in the poodle waste and he fell, kicking the woman's face hard enough to break her nose and snap back her head. A collective shout of surprise and dismay arose from the crowd as the boy scrambled to his knees to attend to her. His friends ran for help.

The old man never fully recovered from the blow to his head. His speech was slurred and he had trouble remembering. His voice would trail off as he thought of his wife and the tragedy of her death from a heart attack beside the healing waters of Lourdes.

Oy! That took an ugly turn didn't it? But it seems to be the end of the story, so what are we doing here?

Well, maybe there is more to the story. What might it be? As Paul Harvey (Look it up!) might have said, "And now, the rest of the story."

You first, but we don't have all day. Go ahead, we'll wait.

?

?

Not so easy, was it?

Well, okay let's see how Arthur….oh, I mean the author...dragged out the denouement. (Oh, while you're looking up Paul Harvey, consider *denouement*, "page two."

(Those who get it will get it.)

If only Mabel had not wanted to sit for a moment in an empty wheelchair—obviously left by someone who had enjoyed a miraculous cure—to watch the panoply of believers while Bert went to buy a souvenir.

Bert had trouble focusing his mind, but it kept chewing at the irony of two people in excellent health who walked to the healing waters of Lourdes and had to be carried out, one never to regain consciousness before dying in a French hospital so far from home and family, the other never regaining the ability to walk or speak clearly.

The leader of the German Boy Scout pack that had thought Lourdes offered the perfect site to do good deeds, quietly resigned his post and left scouting, but his family noticed that he was never again quite the same.

The gate is straight
Deep and wide
Break on through to the other side
Break on through to the other side

"Break on Through (To the Other Side)"
The Doors

Break on Through

David Amalfi awoke gradually, swimming to the surface of consciousness and toward the sound of a tractor harrowing the asparagus field. As the fog cleared, he realized that tractor in his dream was the steady growl of the Amstaff sleeping at the foot of his bed.

As Amalfi became fully conscious, the terrier's growl broke into an enraged bark, allowing the doctor to experience spontaneous momentary levitation.

The dog scrambled to his feet, and bounded to the floor. He ran snarling and barking to the bedroom door, at which he uncharacteristically began to scrabble.

"What's the matter, Max? What is it, boy?"

The dog ignored him, staring intently at the door. In the dull moonlight, David Amalfi could see the hackles standing on his dog's back. At about the same time he heard the muffled staccato pounding on his front door.

The terrier glanced repeatedly at the doctor, impatiently lifting one foot after the other as if standing on a hot surface.

Dr. Amalfi slipped on his robe as he headed for the bedroom door.

Scanning the floor, he could see only one slipper, but the urgent pounding dissuaded him from taking the time to look for the other.

Max raced ahead as they descended the stairs, and stood before the door, barking wildly.

"Easy, Max. It's okay. I'm here."

The furious barking continued unabated.

"It's okay, boy."

"Dr. Amalfi!" an adolescent voice crackled from the other side. "Doctor Amalfi, please!"

Amalfi opened the door to the wide-eyed panicky face of Danny Bourne, a boy who had grown up next door. The pale teenager had a swollen lip, his nose looked broken and one of his eyes was almost shut, with a bloody lump over the eyebrow.

"Danny, what happened?" said the doctor, trying to guide the boy into the house.

"It's mom!" the boy said, pulling away. "You've gotta come quick!"

The boy's voice was thin and reedy; it sounded almost distant as the boy alternated glancing at Amalfi and back into the darkness.

Max, who most often was trying to burrow his nose into Danny's pockets for one of the dog biscuits usually kept there as treats for him, instead took a step back and his hackles went up again. He backed away from the panicky boy, growling deep in his throat.

"What's the matter with him?" the doctor asked, looking from Danny to his dog that continued to slowly back away with a low growl.

"We had a car crash and she's not moving! Please, Doctor Amalfi! You've gotta come now! "

Looking at the boy's terrified face, the doctor grabbed his medical bag from beside the door and quickly slipped barefoot into the cold night. The frosted grass crunched beneath his feet like thin sheets of breaking glass.

"Where?" he asked.

"At the corner," said the boy pulling the doctor by the hand, "Come on!"

The boy's hand felt as if the blood had drained out of it, limp and icy cold.

Hurrying through the night, Doctor Amalfi absently thought that Danny seemed so much younger in his fear than he did when he swaggered by the house with Amie, a girl the thirteen-year-old was trying to impress. Noticing how cold Danny's hand felt, he worried fleetingly about shock.

Danny slipped his hand out of the doctor's and outdistanced the older man in the darkness, Amalfi almost lost sight of the slender youngster, several times. It was like trying to see something that moved at the periphery of your vision in the dark.

His pace stuttered when he saw the car; his anxiety ratcheted up several notches. It didn't look good. The trunk of the car was pointed at the air, like a duck with its head under water. The front end was crumpled against the small boulders that lined the drainage ditch beside the road.

"What happened?" he yelled to the boy who was leaning into the car.

"We were coming home from Gramma's and mom was having trouble staying awake. We were singing with a CD trying to keep her awake, but her head kept jerking forward. I think she fell asleep anyway."

"When we got close to the corner, the car started going faster instead of slowing down. I looked at Mom and she was asleep. So I yelled and grabbed the wheel, but we didn't make the turn. I looked up and saw the tree like it was growing out of our hood and then....."

Amalfi glanced quickly at the tree, an angry gash where the car had apparently scraped its bark away before bouncing into the ditch.

The boy stopped talking as Amalfi raced to the driver's side of the car, where Mary Bourne, Danny's mother and his long-time neighbor and friend, lay with her head on one shoulder, the deflated airbag crumpled in her lap.

Putting his fingers to her throat, he felt for a pulse.

"She's alive! Go to the Martins' house and call 911," Amalfi shouted to the boy. "Hurry."

He called her name and gingerly began trying to assess the woman's condition. When Danny didn't respond and he didn't hear the sound of running feet, Amalfi called to him again.

"Danny? Go call 911!"

Still no answer.

"Danny…?"

Okay, this should come as no surprise to you, but we're just going to put a little hitch in our giddayap here while we try to figure out just what's going on. Oh, sure, Arthur, or whatever you call the guy who wrote this, is looking mighty smug over there because he thinks he has it all figured out, but let's see if we can't puncture that big ego-balloon he has going on.

How would you end this account without boring readers to death?

Already?

Okay, let's see whether Shakespeare here managed to come up with an interesting ending. (Or at least as interesting as yours.)

This
    page
        intentionally
            left
                blank
                    to
                        preserve
                            suspense.

When the doctor raised his eyes to look for the youngster, he saw a passenger in the shotgun seat. The rest of the sentence went unspoken, as the doctor's eyes adjusted to the dark and he tried to discern who the other passenger was. He could see from the angle of the head that the neck appeared broken. His slender young friend, pale and unbreathing, still firmly buckled into his seat belt.

We don't worry about the pennant much

We just like to see the boys hit it deep

There's nothing like the view from the cheap seats.

Alabama

Not the Cheap Seats

The sudden crash and the sound of grinding metal froze Rosaline almost in mid-step. She ran to the front window, fearing the worst.

"Oh, no," she cried. "Not the Ferrari!"

Money wasn't the issue. Exactly. She did all right. Well, at least she did well enough to rub it into the faces of those she had passed on her way up, which is what mattered most to her. With her modest inheritance and her successful law practice, Rosaline had more money than anyone she knew. Anyone she knew in the old neighborhood, anyway. Not that she talked to them or would acknowledge that she knew them. Her life has been a history of quietly clawing her way up, wearing her face of sunny optimism to those above her on the social ladder to conceal the crippling need to amaze and impress the people she grew up with, the people she had scraped off her shoes long ago as she severed ties to her modest roots.

At the country club, where everyone she knew was worth vastly more than she, she knew that she had just slithered in, was on the low end of the scale, but she was a member. In this as in all things, she clung to the superficial trappings of status that accrued to being in the right groups, the right clubs, the right neighborhood. Of course, she had scrabbled into each by a fingernail and membership in each prestigious group was more tenuous than anyone might guess. Behind the show, she was a shell, deeply in debt, shedding those she left behind and alienating those above her on the social scale, those who saw her social-climbing as desperation, those who mocked her intrusion as a pathetic effort to elbow her way into the society of the right people. After cutting herself off from family and friends she didn't think were good enough for her, she found herself sneered at by those who saw her infiltration of their lifestyle an intrusion into a caste of which they had earned entrée by dint of being born into the right families.

In this city, millionaires were not an exclusive club. Hers was the least expensive home in the posh neighborhood, but it was in the neighborhood, in proximity to wealth. Her jewelry was excellent costume jewelry or bargains from distant pawn shops, bazaars, auctions or estate sales. Her designer clothes were purchased from discount houses. The "classic" Ferrari that she had bought at an automobile auction allowed Rosaline to pass among the über rich as one of them, although it cost much less than it appeared. But it was the most authentic of her costly disguises.

She had sunk much more of her "wealth" into the car than she should have but Rosaline was determined to claw her way to the top, and she knew that the only way to get there was to appear to already have arrived. Besides, she loved to flaunt her success, no matter how aware she was that it was a facade.

With the rented art that adorned her walls and the mortgage that reduced her to a quivering mass, she was making the right impression, but she knew how tenuous was her hold on the trappings of wealth.

Being posh had driven Rosaline since she was a girl. She had resented the families that had better cars, better homes, better clothes and better vacations. She had resented her family for not having those things. Her father's car dealership had made him very comfortable, but he was still a car salesman and that shamed her. She was embarrassed that he did not have a college degree, never mind a degree from one of the prestigious schools their neighbors had attended.

But even the most affluent of her neighbors was beneath what she considered her due, her proper station, and she quietly took pride in knowing that she had exploited every opportunity to step on them, to crush them beneath her heel, as she could to rise above them.

Best of all, only the brightest of them understood that she was doing so; she was smarter than them all. She took as her personal motto

Hamlet's observation "that one may smile and smile and be a villain."

She had mastered the act and scorned those stupid enough to buy it. She believed that that included everyone else.

She saw herself as a modern Scarlett O'Hara, except instead of never being hungry again, she vowed never to be upstaged by people who had better pedigrees or made more money. Every relationship she invested in, and every decision she made revolved around how it would affect her social standing, now and in the long run.

At law school she knew that she had found Mr. Right as soon as she realized that the classmate was the scion of one of the most respected and feared law firms in the city. It didn't hurt that he was gorgeous and athletic. In fact, she first was drawn to his smile, which seemed to start in his heart and radiate through his doe-like eyes. Add his self-deprecating humor, kindness, and natural good taste that he wore like comfortable jeans, and he was a catch any way she considered him. More important, he was easy prey.

She pursued him as relentlessly as she could without being obvious. How fortunate that they were in the same study group (how unfortunate that there had been an opening that resulted from another classmate having an unfortunate accident that forced her to drop out for the semester.) How fortunate that it turned out that she loved the same restaurants that he favored, the same music he enjoyed, and the same authors he favored. She was always so lucky, no matter how much effort it required.

How fortunate that he was gallant enough to marry her as soon as she told him, tearful and trembling, that she was carrying his child. She didn't understand how this could happen, she said, apparently lost and bewildered. She had faithfully taken birth-control pills, she said.

And, being a decent fellow he never doubted her.

How unfortunate that she had a miscarriage shortly after their engagement was announced. How he comforted her in her loss, their loss.

How unfortunate that it took so long for him to tumble to the fact that it was a false pregnancy. She had lied.

He had stood by her.

He loved her, he said.

A matter of noblesse oblige, he thought.

How unfortunate that he had died so young – and so tragically in such a freak accident, so soon after Rosaline had been brought into his family's law firm.

63

And now this, she thought, as she ran out to see what had happened to her beloved Ferrari.

The woman standing next to her vehicle–well, now their composite vehicle, as they now appeared to be conjoined—was impeccably dressed. Her perfume was subtle and gently floral. Her expression was well beyond woebegone. Rosaline's dudgeon was somewhat mitigated by the realization that opportunity might have knocked—well, crashed.

As Rosaline approached, the woman looked up and turned her head toward her. "Is it yours?" she asked without preamble.

Ro nodded and her heart fell as she took in the damage to her classic beauty.

"I am so sorry," said the woman, searching though her bag. "I was so excited about good news that my attention wavered."

"Good news?" asked Rosaline absently, as she surveyed the damage with folded arms.

"Yes, and now especially embarrassing, I'm afraid. My husband had just called to tell me that he is about to be appointed state attorney general….My husband!" She dashed to her car and searched around the floor until she came up with a cell phone.

"Daniel? Hello?" she paused. "Oh, no, I am fine darling. I know that it sounded horrible, but it isn't as bad as it sounded. I am so excited for you! And I am so sorry to ruin your news with…"

"Well, no, of course. No. No one was hurt; the other car was parked and no one was in it."

"Yes she is here." She looked up at Rosaline. "You are the owner, you said?" Ro nodded again, studying the woman as her mind raced to determine how best to leverage the opportunity that had just presented itself.

She had been worried that the deductible would wipe her out. The only way that she had been able to afford insurance for the Ferrari was to opt for a ridiculously high deductible. Certainly these people would have insurance that would cover it…and she might make some excellent contacts.

"Of course," she continued into her mobile. "No I have not!" she added with quiet intensity. "It is the middle of the day, Daniel and I have not had anything at all….Of course. Yes, I understand. Yes, I will see you tonight, darling."

She smiled wryly at Rosaline. "He is not pleased with me," she said. "In fact, as I have had a one or two other minor accidents, he would prefer that we not report this to our insurance company, if that is all right with you. She pulled out a card and began writing on its back.

Looking up at Rosaline she smiled. "I always make sure to have a few of my husband's cards with me," she said. "People seem more impressed by a prominent lawyer than a woman whose resume includes only a string of charity work."

She finished writing and her tongue made a soft clucking noise while her head bobbed from side to side as she considered whether she had provided all the necessary information. "I have put my own name and personal contact information on the back of the card. Obviously, I would rather that we handle it between us rather than bothering him with the details."

"Frankly, although he wouldn't say it, I think that he is growing a little tired of my being such a klutz."

She handed the card to Rosaline. "I am Marian, she said. Marian Reilly. This is my cell number so you can always get through to me, and I would love to get this cleared up right away."

"If you will get the repairs made and send me the bill, I will take care of it immediately. I am so embarrassed to cause you the inconvenience….In fact, I would be happy to pay for a rental while yours is being repaired, if you will allow me."

Maybe this would not be so bad, thought Rosaline.

"That is very kind of you," she said. "I would appreciate that."

"Now that I think of it," said Marian, finger to her lips, "I could have the fellow who does our repairs do your work and he could drop off a loaner when he comes to pick it up."

She looked around as if about to share a great secret. "You will understand that—especially now—I am eager to attend to this as quickly as possible with as little fuss as we can manage."

"I do understand" said Rosaline, who had not said so little in as long as she could remember. "I hate to put you out, though."

"Not at all," Marian interrupted. "I appreciate your allowing us to keep this between ourselves."

Marian saw Rosaline look again at her crumpled car. "I will ask Jimmy – the man we use for our body work – to call you as soon as he assesses the damage to tell you how serious he thinks it is and how long he expects the repair work to take. The man is a genius! You won't be able to tell anything happened."

Rosaline looked from the card in her hand to Marian's earnest face. "Of course. Thank you, Mrs. Reilly."

"'Marian,' please. My goodness, we are sharing an experience, after all."

"Marian," she repeated. "Marian Reilly."

"Miss Reilly."

"Marian," she corrected.

"Marian," Rosaline said smiling awkwardly. "Despite the circumstances, I am glad to meet you, Marian. If someone had to wreck my car, I'm glad that it was you."

"Well, I'm afraid that makes one of us," Marian responded wryly.

Marian looked at her watch. "Oh, dear, I am afraid that I am running late. She looked again at the conjoined cars, her Mercedes and Rosaline's Ferrari. "It looks as if your Ferrari got the worst of it," she said. "I think that my bumper just crumpled that rear panel, but the bumper sill looks good."

"Oh." Marian exclaimed. "You know what we should do?" Reaching into her glove box, she extracted a digital camera. "We should take some photos before we do anything else. Even without the insurance company, it makes sense to record the damage for whatever reason." And she started snapping pictures from several different angles, checking them as she went.

"Oh, I even got one of you," she said. "We can compare the expression on your face, before and after the repairs are done."

Rosaline's smile was a disguised grimace.

"Now let me call Jimmy and see how soon he can get here." Scrolling through the numbers in her cell phone, she nodded briefly and pushed the speed dial. While she waited, she looked up at Rosaline. "You don't have to tell me how embarrassing it is to have a body shop on speed dia…. Jimmy?"

"May I speak to him, please? This is Marian Reilly….Thank you."

After a brief pause, Marian's head snapped up. "Jimmy? Jimmy, this is Marian Reilly. I am afraid that I need your help." She paused and listened for a moment. "Yes, I am glad that I could help you to buy your new car, but I need some…special treatment." She paused again to listen and then laughed a throaty laugh.

"Listen, Jimmy, can you work on a Ferrari?"

A pause.

"Of course, I knew you could, I just wanted to be absolutely certain before we went any further." She mugged at Rosaline.

"I'm afraid that I have ruined the back of a lovely old--she saw Rosaline's jaw tighten--a lovely classic Ferrari. The owner has graciously agreed that Daniel and I would pay for it instead of taking all the time to go through insurance."

Another pause.

"Yes, well that might be good news for you, but it probably means keeping my "classic" Mercedes a little longer than I had planned…If Daniel allows me to continue driving."

"I told the owner – her name is Ms Rosaline Tessa – T-e-s-s-a—that we would provide her an appropriate loaner while you are working on her car. Can you arrange for that and deliver the loaner when you pick up her Ferrari? Or if you don't have anything suitable, we can go ahead and rent one."

She listened briefly.

Looking to Rosaline, she said, "He has a Jaguar that he is selling for the owner. If that works for you, he can bring it over right away."

Ro thought briefly before asking "What year?"

"What year?" Reilly repeated into the phone.

"This year? Why is he selling it?"

She listened. Then, laughing, she said, "Must be nice."

Looking to Rosaline she said "His wife hates the color. It is red and she wanted champagne."

Rosaline considered. "A red Jag? Sure, it'll be fun for the interim."

"Wonderful! Okay! That's fine. Thank you, Jimmy. And we'll cover the cost for that as well, for everything, so you won't even need her billing information."

Marian listened for another moment.

"Oh, I see. She said. Just a moment."

"I am so sorry Ms….Rosaline," she continued. "He said that he does need a credit card for insurance purposes."

"He wants my credit card information?"

"I am so sorry. He said that he needs it in case anything happens to the Jaguar while you are driving it."

"I don't know whether I am comfortable with that."

"Oh, I see." She paused. "She is not comfortable with that," she repeated into the telephone. She paused again as if listening. Grimacing she said, "I'm so sorry. He said that he can't take the chance. but he can arrange for a rental, and you can give your credit card information directly to them."

Rosaline pondered a long minute before consenting. "Let me get my purse" she said turning toward the house.,

When she returned, she gave Marian the card so that she could read off the information to Jimmy. She also gave him the address and listened for a moment before disconnecting.

"He said that he can be here in about a half-hour. I am so glad that this will work out! I want you to have as little inconvenience as possible."

She looked again at her watch. "Oh, my! I am so late!" She returned her gaze to Ro.

"Rosaline, I hate to appear rude, but this is very important for my husband and Jimmy is on his way. Would you mind if I were to leave you alone?"

She saw Rosaline's uncertainty and added: "You have my cell number – and let me give you Jimmy's number." She scrolled through her directory again and read the number to Rosaline, who wrote it under Marian's number on her husband's card.

Marian smiled and returned Rosaline's pen. "Thank you, Rosaline. You have made what could have been an unpleasant situation an example of how civilized people can behave."

"You have made it very easy," said Ro.

"I caused the problem, "Marian continued. "The least I can do is try to take as much of the burden as possible from your shoulders."

Rosaline followed her to the car and watched as Marian gently reversed from where she had implanted her bumper in Rosaline's Ferrari. She was surprised at how little the collision had damaged the Mercedes, and looking at her own car realized that the damage was contained to one panel. The horrendous sound of the collision seemed entirely out of proportion to the actual damage.

"Does it look as if anything is rubbing on the tire?" asked Marian..

Rosaline hastened to look at the front tires. "No, you are good."

"Wonderful," said Marian. "Thank you for being so understanding, dear."

"You're welcome Marian. I hope that I will be able to meet your husband."

"My husband? Why on earth would you want to meet him?"

Rosaline laughed. "I guess that I didn't mention that I'm a lawyer as well. I would be honored to meet the next attorney general."

"Aah," said Rosaline. "Another one of those....Now I am as surprised as I am relieved that we could settle this so quickly."

"Of course, I would be happy to get the two of you together; it's the least that I could do."

As she drove off, the two women waved to each other as if they were old friends, Rosaline's mind already racing to calculate how she could capitalize on the incident.

Waiting for Jimmy, Rosaline grew increasingly uneasy. He seemed to be taking much longer than Matrian had indicated, but just as she was about to call to check on him, she saw a bright red Jaguar pull up in front of her house, followed closely by a large flatbed truck.

Exhaling a breath she didn't know she had been holding, she went to meet the body man and collect the key to the Jag from its driver. She almost dropped it when it caught on the driver's glove, but she caught it in the air and smiled at the man who delivered it. She watched him help Jimmy gently load her Ferrari on the back of the truck and felt a sudden sadness as she watched them drive off with it.

But... she had the use of a cherry Jaguar and she could look forward to meeting the state's next attorney general.

Rosaline was eager to take the Jag through its paces on the way to the office.

Hold it right there!
While Rosaline is putting the Jag through its paces, let's give s
situation some thought.
It seems as if this presumptuous social-climbing snob l the breaks.
So, what happens?
Take your time.
Dum te dum dum dum.

Really, That's all you have? Let's just go on, then.

This
    page
       intentionally
      left
        blank
         to
          preserve
           suspense

Rosaline was eager to take the Jag through its paces on the way to the office. She was going a few miles over the speed limit when she spotted the police car coming up steadily in her rear view mirror.

Immediately easing off the gas to return to the speed limit, she was dismayed to see the police lights begin flashing at her rear bumper. She was more dismayed to see a second police car coming up fast.

She pulled over to the side of the road and saw the driver of the first car approach her with his hand resting lightly on his gun.

"Driver, step out of the car and keep your hands where I can see them."

Rosaline hesitated. This is not the way a police officer typically responds to a car going a few miles over the speed limit. In fact, Rosaline believed that there was a tacit agreement between police and drivers that the speed limit really meant three or four miles above whatever is posted.

"Driver, step out of the car now and keep your hands where I can see them."

She saw a second police officer moving stealthily along the off-road side of the car and opened her door.

"Easy," said the first office. "Come out slowly with your hands in plain sight."

She did as directed, but as soon as she was standing, the first officer said "Face the car and place your hands on the top."

"Officer, what is this…?"

Her question was aborted in mid-sentence as the policeman slammed her against the side of the Jag.

"There is no reason for…"

"Quiet!"

She felt his hands briskly checking her for weapons as a second officer opened the passenger door and began searching the car.

"Officer. I did not give permission to search my car. I am a lawyer and I do not give you permission."

The policeman smiled cruelly. "If it was yours, we'd need it, but not for a car that is reported stolen."

"Stolen?"

She began to turn toward him.

"Keep your hands on the car," said the first officer as he slammed her against it again.

"Officer, obviously there is a mistake. This car is a loaner while my car is being repaired."

"'Loaner,' hunh?"

"License is clean," said his partner.

"You see, Officer," said Rosaline, turning toward him.

"Yeah, I see. First time you got caught," said the officer as he guided his patrol car and covered her head as he helped her roughly into the back seat.

Waiting in the back seat while the police officers thoroughly searched the car, under the seats, in the door and seat pockets, and the trunk, Rosaline was bewildered.

Another flatbed truck arrived and the this time it was the Ferrari that was loaded on as Rosaline protested that this misunderstanding could be cleared up if the officer would only call "Jimmy."

"Tell you what, lady, why don't you call him if you want, but you'd be smarter to call your lawyer."

"I am a lawyer," she protested

"Then I guess you knew that already."

Rosaline was dismayed and confused when she learned that Jimmy's number was a prepaid phone, no longer in use. She was astonished to learn that the number Marian had given her was invalid as well. And embarrassed to realize that the attorney general's wife had been visiting family at the time of their "accident"….and she had a different surname…and broken-hearted to learn that the Jaguar was indeed stolen and her beloved Ferrari was gone without a trace. Probably sold for parts, the police said when they learned that she really had a Ferrari registered to her. But even when they released her, she could tell that they still didn't believe her story about the Jaguar.

Worst of all was the next morning when she saw her mug shot in the newspaper with an article about a "Local Lawyer Charged with Grand Theft Auto." She was stunned at how much personal information could be gleaned in such a brief time. And how many people saying unkind things about her could surface so quickly.

Gone with her Ferrari was her reputation, her image, and the house of cards she had sacrificed so much and so many to build.

Sickened by the article about her, she turned quickly to the employment pages. The partners in her firm had made clear that they couldn't afford the association with her.

ABOUT THE AUTHOR

Craig Lancto is a veteran teacher and journalist, who taught high school English, journalism, and drama for more than 20 years. In the early-80s he began contributing to a variety of publications, mainly on topics relating to education. For 15 years he wrote a weekly opinion column for a number of newspapers in the Metropolitan DC area and hosted radio and cable television talk-shows that focused on educational issues.

By the mid-90s, Craig permanently traded chalk for a pen, when he became a full-time freelance writer and editor. That changed in the late 90s when he was offered a position at *The Washington Times*, where he coordinated educational programs, consulted with local school systems, taught media literacy, and published either three half-pages or two full pages a week on issues relating to education.

His educational guides and tabloids have been used not only by *The Washington Times,* but also many other newspapers throughout the country.

In 2002, he eagerly accepted the position of education editor at *The World & I* magazine, where he remained until the magazine's 18-year run ended in 2005, at which time he returned to freelancing and writing and editing special publications for *The Washington Times*. Between 2005 and 2009 he served as executive editor at the Sun Newspapers of Alexandria and the *Alexandria Times*. From 2009 to 2012 he served as deputy chief of outreach and director of communications and media relations at the Near East South Asia Center for Strategic Studies.

Since 2014, he has lived in Virginia's Shenandoah Valley, where he writes, kayaks, and foments general mischief.

craiglancto@gmail.com

www.ingramcontent.com/pod-product-compliance
Lightning Source LLC
Chambersburg PA
CBHW071345130626
46556CB00005B/2042